# Meg Mac...

and

# The Mystery on
# Main Street

## A Solve-It-Yourself Mystery

by  Lucinda Landon

Secret Passage Press
Tucker Hollow   North Scituate
Rhode Island

Books by Lucinda Landon
*Meg Mackintosh and the Case of the Missing Babe Ruth Baseball*
*Meg Mackintosh and the Case of the Curious Whale Watch*
*Meg Mackintosh and the Mystery at the Medieval Castle*
*Meg Mackintosh and the Mystery at Camp Creepy*
*Meg Mackintosh and the Mystery in the Locked Library*
*Meg Mackintosh and the Mystery at the Soccer Match*
*Meg Mackintosh and the Mystery on Main Street*
*American History Mysteries*

# Copyright @ 2000 by Lucinda Landon

For information:
Secret Passage Press, 26 Tucker Hollow, N. Scituate, Rhode Island 02857

## First Edition

Library of Congress Control Number Data
Landon, Lucinda.
    Meg Mackintosh and the Mystery on Main Street: a solve-it-yourself mystery/ by Lucinda Landon. - 1st. ed.
    Summary: A big holiday storm is looming and a baffling mystery is building. Meg's brother has lost a priceless family heirloom somewhere along Main Street. The reader may search the pictures for key clues to solve the case along with Meg.
(1. Mystery and detective stories.  2. Literary recreations)


Library of Congress Control Number: 00-092660

ISBN 1-888695-06-4

10 9 8 7 6 5 4 3 2 1

PRINTED IN THE UNITED STATES OF AMERICA

For Dorothy, Charles, and Richard
And in memory of Edward

## December 22

"Meg, you've got to help me!" Peter called as he pounded on his sister's door and stumbled into her room.

Meg leaned back in her chair and gave Peter a long look. "Let's see, I detect that you've been shopping at the camera store, had a close encounter with a holly bush, and spilled stuff on your jacket," Meg observed. "It also looks as though you've lost a mitten, and maybe something else, since you're so upset. How am I doing so far?"

"Pretty good, Sherlock," Peter replied. "But listen, this is serious. I did lose something, and I'm in big trouble if I don't find it. You're the ace detective. You've got to help me find it."

Meg took out her notebook and pen. "Peter, start at the beginning, tell me exactly what happened."

5

Peter dropped his bag on the floor and stretched out on Meg's bed. "I went over to Gramps' house after school," Peter began. "He asked me to run some errands—pick up a mystery novel he'd ordered at the Book Nook, go to the florist for some holly, and take a ring to the jewelry store to be cleaned."

"Wait a minute—what kind of ring?" Meg asked.

"Well, old. It was his grandmother's. It's gold with rubies and diamonds, so I'm sure it's worth a lot of money. But to Gramps it's a priceless antique."

Meg had a sinking feeling. "Let me guess: You lost the ring? Or maybe it was stolen?"

"Yeah, it's awful. Gramps wanted the ring polished at the jewelers so he could it to give to

Mom for Christmas. I told him I'd be especially careful and now look what happened," said Peter with a heavy sigh. "If I don't find the ring, I'll ruin Christmas for Gramps, Mom, and me."

"And maybe me, too," Meg muttered under her breath. "This does sound pretty bad."

"It's hopeless," Peter moaned. "The ring was in a little white jewelry box. I'll never find it on Main Street, especially during the holidays."

Skip, their dog, jumped on the bed to console him.

"Pull yourself together, Peter," said Meg. "I'll help you solve this, but I need more details. Exactly where did you go after you left Gramps' house?"

"I went straight to Main Street. I saw Zeke and Zack building a snowman in front of their house, so I helped them for a minute."

"Where was the ring? Did you put it down while you were making the snowman?" Meg quizzed him.

"I carried it inside my mitten, so I could feel the box the whole time," replied Peter.

"And you probably wouldn't have taken off your mittens while making a snowman," Meg commented.

"I don't think so," Peter looked anguished.

"Was their older sister Becky there?" Meg asked.

"No, but they told me she was helping at the bakery next door," Peter continued. "So I went there, just to say hi."

"Okay, now think back to the bakery," Meg commanded, trying to get her brother to visualize the scene. "Tell me what was going on."

"Becky was stirring batter for a big batch of gingerbread, and I—" Peter stammered, blushing. "I took out the box and showed her the ring," Peter confessed. "Then I went to the bookstore and the florist, but when I got to the jewelers, I realized I didn't have the ring."

"Okay, that's a good start to the investigation," she said, writing The Mystery on Main Street at the top of her notebook page. "Now, empty your pockets. There might be some clues in them."

**What do you deduce from the contents of Peter's pockets?**

"Ah, ha! Here's a receipt for two donuts and a hot chocolate—so you stayed at the bakery for a snack, and that's probably what you spilled on your jacket." Her eyes widened as she unfolded another piece of paper. "Hey, these are instructions for a new camera! Did you buy something for yourself right before Christmas?"

"Meg, I've been saving up for that camera," Peter tried to explain. "My old one broke, and I'm planning to make prints for Christmas presents."

Meg gave him a dubious look and continued. "Peter, if you want me to help, you've got to tell me the whole story. Now, when did you buy the camera?"

"The camera store is the first place I went— before Zeke and Zack's house." Peter said humbly.

Meg shook her head. She studied the other items from Peter's pockets and jotted in her notebook.

The Mystery on
Main Street
Clues in Peter's pockets:
1) Film holder⎫ Camera
   instructions⎭ Store
2) Receipt- Bakery
3) Bookmark- Book Nook
4) Holly- Florist
5) Coins- sticky from
         hot chocolate

"Peter, was Aunt Alice at the Book Nook by any chance?" Meg asked. "Gramps told me she's working there while she visits during the holidays."

"Yes, in fact I paid her for Gramps' book," Peter answered.

"And?" Meg urged him on. "Anything else?"

"She yelled at me for giving her a ten dollar bill that was all sticky with hot chocolate," Peter admitted. "You'd think she'd give me a break since we're related."

"You know Aunt Alice better than that," said Meg,

"Do you think she took the ring?" Peter gasped. "She's always up to something."

Just then their father called from downstairs, "Peter! Meg! Time for dinner!"

"Remember, mum's the word," Meg advised Peter on their way downstairs. "But there's one thing you have to do tonight."

**What do you think Meg wants Peter to do?**

"The film container in your pocket was empty. That suggests that you had already loaded the new camera, and were snapping pictures that might hold an important clue," Meg whispered to Peter as their parents sat down at the dining room table. "I need to see them as soon as possible."

"You're right—I'll develop the film tonight," muttered Peter.

"What was that, Peter?" their mother asked. "You're going to work in the darkroom tonight? Great, could you make some prints of last year's archeological dig in Greece—I need them for a proposal for a new expedition."

"Where are you planning to go next? Egypt? Chile?" Dad asked.

"The excavation sites won't be decided until spring. For now, I'll just be discovering treasures

on Main Street," Mom laughed.

What does she mean by *that*? Meg thought to herself. She tried to change the subject. "How are things in the math department, Dad?"

"Better than ever as of one o-clock today, because the college closed for vacation," Dad joked. "I finally had time for some Christmas shopping this afternoon. I saw Aunt Alice on Main Street. Don't forget, she and Gramps have invited us over for cookies on the afternoon before Christmas."

"Where did you see Aunt Alice?" Meg asked.

"She was coming out of the jewelry store," Dad replied. He smiled mischievously. "She said she had a little surprise for you two. Something about an old family treasure."

"Really?" said Meg, kicking Peter's foot under the table. Could Alice have the ring? she wondered.

Where Peter went
on Main Street:
1) Gramps' house
2) Camera store
3) Zeke + Zack's
4) Bakery
5) Book Nook
6) Florist
7) Jewelers

Meg worked on her notes while Peter developed the film in the dark room. After a while, she knocked on the darkroom door. "Peter are you done yet? Can I come in?"

"Yeah, it's okay." Peter opened the door and flicked on the lights. "I just hung the film to dry, but I won't have prints until tomorrow."

"I guess I can wait," said Meg. "There are other things I can investigate tomorrow on my way to school."

"Where are you going first? Not Gramp's house I hope. I don't want him to suspect that

14

something's wrong." Peter looked at Meg's notes. "Do you think you'll have to smash down Zeke and Zack's snowman to look for the ring?"

"You're wrong about that, Peter." Meg replied. "But maybe I should go to the camera store and return your camera. Then you'll have some money to replace the ring."

"Meg, you wouldn't!" exclaimed Peter.

"No, Peter. I intend to find the ring," said Meg confidently. "And I know where I'm going to start."

**Why was Peter wrong about smashing the snowman? Where was Meg going?**

## December 23

Meg walked past Main Street every day on her way to and from school. This morning, she stopped to observe the setting of the mystery. She saw the snowman, but she knew that the ring wasn't lost in the snow, or at the camera store, because Peter still had it at the bakery when he showed it to Becky.

Meg quickly sketched a map of Main Street, being sure to put all the stores in the right order. She knew the bakery would be the only store open that early.

"I think I have time to do a little investigating," Meg said to herself, as she felt in her pocket for some change. "And time to get a little snack before school."

Mrs. Roberts, the baker was putting the finishing touches on a gingerbread house when Meg entered the cinnamon-scented shop.

"Hi, Mrs. Roberts. Wow! That house looks too pretty to eat!" said Meg.

"Thanks, Meg. I love decorating with all of these candies and sugar crystals...they sparkle like diamonds, don't they!" Mrs. Roberts exclaimed.

Meg was startled at the mention of diamonds and looked carefully at the glittering, candy roof.

"Can I get you something?" Mrs. Roberts asked.

"I'll have one of those cinnamon buns, please," Meg replied. "I was wondering—did you see Peter in here yesterday afternoon?"

"Yes, Peter was here. How could I forget? He spilled hot chocolate all over," Mrs. Robert's wiped icing from her brow.

"Would you remember seeing a small square jewelry box that Peter had with him?" Meg asked.

18

"Yes, I do. I think he showed Becky what was inside. Maybe Peter's got a crush on her," Mrs. Roberts smiled.

Meg paid for the bun and thought about the big batch of batter, and how clumsy Peter is when he's flustered. "Did you make this gingerbread house out of yesterday's batter?"

"No, we made gingerbread men with that batch. I sent them all over to your school for today's holiday party." She returned to her decorating.

Meg sat down at a little round table and jotted in her notebook while she nibbled on the bun.

"Hmmm, there are lots of possibilities, and I'm just getting started." Meg looked at her watch. "Uh, oh, I'd better get going to school."

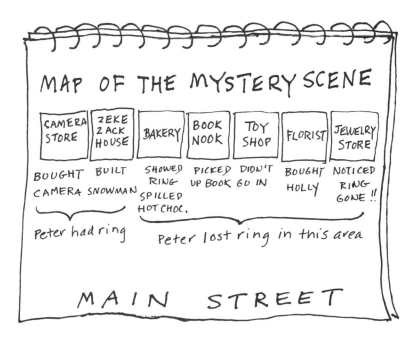

MAP OF THE MYSTERY SCENE

| CAMERA STORE | ZEKE ZACK HOUSE | BAKERY | BOOK NOOK | TOY SHOP | FLORIST | JEWELRY STORE |
|---|---|---|---|---|---|---|
| BOUGHT CAMERA | BUILT SNOWMAN | SHOWED RING SPILLED HOT CHOC. | PICKED UP BOOK | DIDN'T GO IN | BOUGHT HOLLY | NOTICED RING GONE !! |

Peter had ring     Peter lost ring in this area

MAIN STREET

It was the last day of school before vacation. Meg's classroom was having a Winter Holiday Party celebrating festivals from around the world. Mrs. Wong, Simon's mom, was at school that day helping out and collecting canned goods donated to needy families. She had Simon's two-year-old brother, Eric, with her.

"Wouldn't you know, my mom had to bring my little brother to the party," Simon complained to his friend Nick. "He's always making a scene. You should have heard him screaming at the toyshop yesterday when he saw Santa. It was so embarrassing."

"Hi, Meg. Would you like a gingerbread man?"

asked Simon's mom. "I saw your brother on Main Street yesterday. He was nice enough to take some photos of Eric for me."

"That's nice," Meg said. She took a bite of the gingerbread man, thinking hard about the clues so far. Suddenly Eric started screaming and knocked over a plate of cookies.

"Quick, give him something to do!" Simon jumped in. "Have him stack these cans and boxes— it's the only thing that makes him stop crying!"

Meg stared at her notes. "Hey, Nick and Simon, there's something I need you to do for me, and I don't think you'll mind."

**What does Meg want Nick and Simon to do?**

"I need you to eat the rest of these gingerbread men and make sure that you don't swallow a ring that might have been cooked inside—I'll explain later. And make sure no one else in the class finds it."

They looked at Meg quizzically.

"Not a bad job," said Nick.

"As long as we don't chip our teeth," said Simon as he grabbed a handful of gingerbread men.

Meg's best friend Liddy came over. "Meg, what's going on? It sounds as though you're trying to solve a case."

Meg pulled Liddy aside. "I am on a case—a mystery on Main Street. Peter lost a valuable ruby and diamond ring and I have to find it before Christmas. Can you help me after school?" Meg pleaded.

"A mystery on Main Street! I love it! What do we have to do? Do you think someone stole the ring? Do you have any suspects?" Liddy gazed at Meg's notes.

SUSPECTS:
Who saw the ring?
Becky        ?
Mrs. Roberts    ?
Aunt Alice     ?
Florist   ?
Mom     ?
Dad    ?
Jeweler ?

Meg told Liddy the facts of the case as they set off to the Book Nook to question Aunt Alice.

"Hello, dearest dears." Alice greeted them. "Did you come to see what I wanted for Christmas?"

'That's it, Aunt Alice." Meg glanced at Liddy. "You're the only one left on my list."

"Jewels, my dear, jewels and books. They're the only things I really treasure anymore," Alice said with a twinkle. "Be sure to mention that to your Grandfather. He has some old family heirlooms I'm hoping he finally wants to part with."

Liddy gave Meg a curious look.

Aunt Alice
Motives:
1) Loves jewels
2) Wants family heirlooms
3) Books on gems
4) Acts suspicious

Meg ignored her and asked Aunt Alice about the previous afternoon. "Did Peter leave anything here yesterday when he picked up Gramps' book?"

"No, no, I'm sure he didn't. He was very busy loading film in his camera. All he left behind was some wrappers, which I threw away, and his sticky money," answered Alice, somewhat testily, as she looked at her watch. "Oh, heavens! Look at the time. I'm off work now, and I have lots to do." Alice dashed for the door, grabbing her coat, purse, and books.

"That was an awfully quick exit," said Liddy.

"She does seem suspicious," Meg commented as she jotted in her notebook.

"Now where do we go?" asked Liddy.

**Where would you go next?**

Meg and Liddy paused on Main Street before they went into the florist shop. It had started to snow.

"It's hard to suspect people during the holidays, especially my own relatives," Meg confided to Liddy. "Why, I even suspected my own mother of finding the ring, when she joked during dinner about excavating on Main Street."

"Meg, remember what you always say—a good detective is suspicious of everyone," Liddy told her. "And on that wise note, I have to get home now. We're celebrating Hanukkah tonight."

"Oh, I almost forgot," said Meg as she took a package out of her knapsack and gave it to Liddy. "Happy Hanukkah!"

26

Liddy unwrapped the present. "A magnifying glass!" she exclaimed. "Thanks, Meg, it's just what I wanted." She gave her a hug. "Why don't you wait and open your present on Christmas. Here, put it under your tree."

"Okay," Meg promised. "You'd better get going— and be sure to call me if you find any clues on the way home!"

"Well, I did notice something suspicious when I compared your notes about where Peter went yesterday with all the stores on Main Street." Liddy suggested.

**Look again at Meg's sketch of the Main Street stores. What did Liddy find suspicious?**

"I can't believe Peter went into all these stores and didn't go into the toy store. It's just not like Peter," Liddy commented. "He loves toys and gadgets."

"You're right, that is strange" Meg agreed.

"Meg, look, there's the florist." Liddy nudged her. "He's locking up his store. You'd better catch him."

Meg waved goodbye to Liddy and caught up with the florist. "Mr. Drum! It's me, Meg Mackintosh. My brother Peter was in your shop yesterday, buying holly. I was wondering if he left anything there?"

"As a matter of fact, Peter did drop something. I was going to give it to your Mom. I've seen her a lot on Main Street lately," said Mr. Drum as he pulled something from his coat pocket.

Meg's eyes widened with anticipation.

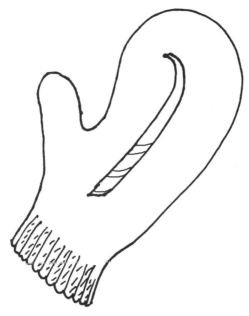

"Oh, it's Peter's mitten." Meg took it and quickly checked to see if the jewelry box was still inside. Alas, it was empty. "Thanks," she said. Could Mr. Drum have taken the ring? She sat down on a street bench and looked over her notes. A few minutes later she saw Mr. Drum coming out of the toy store and he locked that door, too! Then he went into the jewelry store.

Meg's notes were getting soggy from snowflakes. Everyone is looking suspicious! she thought as she packed up her things. Then she noticed a skinny white stick stuck to Peter's mitten. Hmm, what is this? she wondered. It smells like peppermint.

**Do you have any ideas what's stuck to Peter's mitten? What does the clue mean?**

Meg examined the stick. It had a slight curve to it. It's a candy cane with all the stripes licked off, she deduced. She carefully folded the mitten back around the candy cane. "Evidence to show Peter," she muttered as she headed home.

She found Peter in his room and pulled out the mitten to show him. "Peter, look what Mr. Drum, the florist, found."

Peter looked up. "You're kidding! You found it!"

"No, I'm not kidding. He found your mitten in his shop. But the ring box wasn't inside." Meg showed him. "And this candy cane was stuck to it. Come on, Peter. Something about your story doesn't add up! You didn't tell me you went in the

toy store. That's where they were giving away free candy canes. Why didn't you tell me?"

"I didn't tell you because I went in there to get you a Christmas present," Peter explained. "Look, I was going to tell you tonight, when I showed you these photos."

"Is there a picture of my present?" Meg asked slyly.

"No. And I still didn't get you anything," Peter said sheepishly. "But I will tomorrow. Now take a look."

"I can make at least one deduction," Meg declared.

**What has Meg deduced?**

"I deduce that you lost the ring between the bakery and the florist, because you showed it to Becky at the bakery, it wasn't in the gingerbread batter, and the mitten was empty at the florist." Meg drew on her map. "Now let me see the photos you took."

"I only shot a few," Peter told her. "I saw Simon, his mom, and little brother in front of the toy store. I took a picture of them outside, and then their

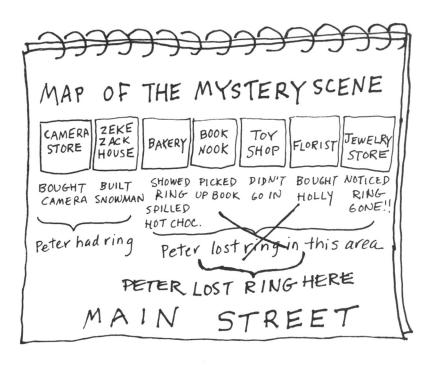

mom wanted me to go inside to take a picture of Eric with Santa. Eric threw a fit."

"Hmm, every picture tells a story," said Meg. "I'm just not sure how the story turns out. I do know that you took your mittens off."

**Do you see anything unusual
in Peter's photos?
Why would Peter have taken
the mitten off?**

"Peter if you took pictures in the toy store, you probably took your mittens off so you could press the buttons easier," said Meg, as she examined the photos.

"Look, you can see one of your mittens lying on the floor, and that looks like the ring box sticking out. And look at this photo with the hand reaching towards something. Whose hand is it?"

"It's Santa's hand, silly! He was reaching for the candy canes to give away," Peter laughed. "Great, now you suspect Santa!"

"I have to suspect everyone," Meg insisted. "And why was Eric crying?" she asked.

"He was scared, I guess," said Peter. "He started screaming. Only Simon could get him to stop."

Mom poked her head in the door. "Come on, you two. I made some popcorn to string and hang on the tree."

"That only takes forever," mumbled Peter.

"In that case, I have another special job just for you, Peter," said Mom as she headed down the stairs.

"Uh, oh," said Peter. "I guess the mystery is on hold 'til tomorrow, Meg-O. Only one more day to solve this."

"Thanks for the Christmas *pressure*," said Meg.

"Gramps hinted that he has something very special for me this year," Mom told Dad.

"Don't get your hopes up, dear. He has told me that every year since I was ten. One year my special present was a file cabinet."

"That sure sounds like fun," said Peter, as he untangled a long string of Christmas tree lights.

"Actually, I'm very attached to that file cabinet. I keep my math worksheets in it," said Dad.

"I've got a math problem for you, Dad," said Meg.

36

"If I can fit three kernels of popcorn on this needle, how long will it take me to finish this bowl?"

"Just keep stringing, Meg-O. And it's not fair to eat the popcorn as you go along," Mom teased. "Skip can have a little though."

"Look at all the snow that's fallen," said Dad. "We're supposed to get a big storm."

"A real white Christmas!" Mom said excitedly.

Just what I need, a blizzard on Main Street, with snow covering every clue, thought Meg.

## December 24

"Due to the heavy snow accumulation, many local stores have called the station to say they'll be closing early, so I hope everyone's shopping is done!" chirped the radio announcer.

"Rats!" said Meg as she turned off her clock radio and looked out her window. "There's a ton of snow."

Peter knocked on her door. "Come on, Meg, we have some shoveling to do."

When they had finished, it was time to go over to Gramps' house. "Don't forget to bring the boughs of holly," Meg reminded Peter.

Aunt Alice greeted them at the door. "Welcome, dearests! Have some eggnog and get ready to sing!"

The family sang carols while Alice played the piano, but Meg couldn't help thinking about the lost ring and how little time was left to find it. When they started to sing the Twelve Days of Christmas, Aunt Alice winked at Meg and then lingered on the line "*F-I-I-V-E G-O-O-L-D-E-N R-I-N-G-S.*"

"Aunt Alice, were you hinting at something when you were singing about the gold rings?" Meg asked, boldly.

"I know that *somebody* is getting a special ring tomorrow" Alice whispered.

"You do? How do you know?" Meg stared at her.

"Don't tell anyone," Aunt Alice continued. "But I saw a ring in a box in Peter's mitten at the Book Nook. He was so busy loading his camera, he didn't see me peek at it."

"Did you put the ring and box back in the mitten, Aunt Alice?" asked Meg.

"Of course I did, dear. I wouldn't want to ruin a Christmas surprise."

"Oh, you'll still be surprised, Aunt Alice," Meg told her with a smile.

While they drove home Meg studied her notes.

Alice saw the ring at the bookstore...that really narrows the possibilities, Meg thought to herself as she pulled out Peter's photographs.

Then Peter suddenly burst out, "Mom, Dad you've got to drop Meg and me off! We can walk home."

**Where does Peter want to be dropped off?**

"On Main Street, of course," said Peter, as Mom pulled the car over. "I have some last-minute shopping to do," said Peter as they jumped out.

"Isn't it a little late?" said Dad. "Everything's going to be closed."

"Some stores might be open—it's still early on Christmas Eve," Meg said, trying to keep from sounding too desperate.

"Okay," said Mom. "See you in a while."

"Thanks for having them stop, Peter. Come on, we're going to the florist." Meg pulled his sleeve.

"What for?" Peter asked her. "Forget about finding the ring. I'm telling Gramps that I lost it. I've decided to go to the camera store, assuming

it's open. I'm going to return my camera, get the money back, buy Mom a nice present, and something for you, too."

"Don't worry about me, Peter," said Meg as she gazed at the stores on Main Street. "But listen, the pieces of this puzzle are falling into place."

"What do you mean, Meg?" said Peter as he yanked on the toy store door. "Rats!" exclaimed Peter. "This place is locked up for the night."

"Mr. Drum, the florist, is still open next door. Let's go see him."

**What is Meg getting at?**
**Do you know where the ring is?**

"Mr. Drum, Peter lost something in the toy store and he really needs it tonight, but it's closed. I saw you locking the doors last night. Do you still have a key?" asked Meg

"Of course, my daughter owns the shop. Come on, I'll let you in." Mr. Drum said helpfully.

"Meg, what is it? Do you know where the ring is?" asked Peter as they were about to enter the toyshop.

"Before we go in, let me explain. Alice just told me that she saw the ring, in the box, in your mitten when you left the Book Nook," Meg told them. "Then you came to the toyshop, took off your mittens and threw them and your other stuff on the floor. While you were taking Eric's picture with Santa, he started screaming, just like at the school party."

"What does Eric have to do with it?" asked Peter.

"In order to get him to stop crying, Simon says Eric likes to stack blocks. Look at the edge of this photo—you can see Eric stacking." Meg showed the photos to a curious Mr. Drum.

Meg pointed to the toy store window. "And here is where he stacked the jewelry box. The alphabet blocks usually spell 'toyshop'—see the photo before you went in. But now, the blocks say 'YOPHTOS' and there's one extra white block—it's the jewelry box! Eric found it on the floor, mixed it up with the other blocks and stacked it." They went into the toyshop, and Meg took the box from the stack and handed it Peter.

Peter opened the jewelry box to discover the ring was still in it. "Meg, you're a genius!"

"Thank you," said Meg. "And thank you, Mr. Drum."

## December 25

"Gramps, what a beautiful ring!" Mom hugged him.

"He gave me an emerald bracelet," shrilled Alice. "George, you sweetie."

"You only gave me a hundred hints," said Gramps.

"Here's an old treasure for you and Peter," Alice gave it to Peter. "It's an antique Parcheesi board. It was Gramps' and mine when we were kids."

"It's great," said Peter.

"I love it," Meg thanked Aunt Alice. So that's why she was acting so suspicious, Meg thought to herself. "Look what Liddy gave me—a new notebook for my next mystery." She showed them.

"Great," said Dad. "I hope you have a new case pretty soon. You haven't had much to solve lately."

Meg and Peter looked at each other and laughed.

**Happy Holidays to all
from the Mackintosh's!**

Looking for more Meg Mackintosh?
Visit www.megmackintosh.com.

## About the author

Lucinda Landon has always loved mysteries. She has also always loved to draw. After studying art at the Rhode Island School of Design, she illustrated *The Young Detective's Handbook*, by William Vivian Butler. That book received a special Edgar Allan Poe Award from the Mystery Writers of America and it launched Meg Mackintosh, who soon starred in her own adventures. The Meg Mackintosh Mystery series is now seven books strong, all published by Secret Passage Press. Meg and her brother Peter also appear in *American History Mysteries*, which Ms. Landon wrote and illustrated. Lucinda Landon lives in Rhode Island with her husband, photographer Jim Egan, and their sons Alex and Eric. Their 1700's home has a hiding place behind the chimney and several trap doors leading to a secret passage.

Lucinda Landon at about the same age as Meg Mackintosh.